CAMILLA GRYSKI

Cat's Cradle and Other String Games #2

INTRODUCTION 2

ABOUT THE
STRING 3

TERMINOLOGY 6

THE
FISH SPEAR 14
Be equipped for fishing.

WINKING EYE 16
Use your imagination but don't blink!

THE SAW 18
Saw back and forth and chant the Scottish verse.

THE FLY 20
Try to catch him before he flies away.

THE HOGAN
AND THE BUNCH
OF BANANAS 22
Pitch your tent, then pick a banana.

MAN
ON A BED 24
When the bed breaks, the man falls out!

A BIRD 26
This bird actually flies!

MAN CLIMBING
A TREE 28
The higher he climbs, the smaller he gets.

THE
GIANT
CLAM 30
Seesaw your hands and the clam will open and shut.

APACHE
DOOR 32
Weave a beautifully patterned tent flap.

CAT'S
CRADLE 1 37
Making the cradle.

CAT'S
CRADLE 2 38
From a cradle to a soldier's bed.

CAT'S
CRADLE 3 39
From a soldier's bed to candles.

CAT'S
CRADLE 4 40
When the flames die down, sleep in a manger.

CAT'S
CRADLE 5 41
Glittering diamonds!

CAT'S
CRADLE 6 42
The diamonds shine in the cat's eye.

CAT'S
CRADLE 7 43
This fish dish has a mystery figure.

CAT'S
CRADLE 8 44
Make two royal crowns and end the game.

CAT'S
CRADLE 9 45
Beat your own drum!

CAT'S
CRADLE 10 46
It's back to diamonds.

CAT'S
CRADLE 11 47
A Japanese fairy tale — don't be left holding the string!

ILLUSTRATED BY:
TOM SANKEY

ANGUS & ROBERTSON PUBLISHERS

Introduction

The more string games I learn, the more fascinated I become with the art of weaving patterns, creating birds and animals, and making magic with my fingers and a loop of string.

String figures, or cat's cradles, are part of the culture of many native peoples, and are probably one of the oldest games in the world. They were used to illustrate stories, to pass on traditions and, of course, to amuse and amaze.

The people who created these string patterns used different materials: left-over fishing line, braided hair, and sinew. They may have worked out their designs in snow houses in the Arctic or on beaches in the South Pacific, but they were all artists in string who delighted in conjuring up beautiful pictures with a loop that could be kept in a pocket or around a wrist.

String figures must be shared if they are to be preserved. We are indebted to the anthropologists who patiently learned and recorded string games so that we can learn and teach them today.

In this book you will find different kinds of string figures. There are patterns, tricks, moving figures and some games to play with your friends.

The easier figures are near the beginning of the book. It's best to try these first before going on to figures that have more steps and trickier moves. When you have learned a figure, do it several times, and then your fingers will remember it for you.

By learning and sharing these string games, you will become part of a tradition that links people all over the world — and you'll have a lot of fun!

The spirit of cat's cradles came to Eskimo children who played at string figures late at night. The spirit made a strange sound like the crackling of dry skins and challenged the maker of string figures to a race, to see who could make Opening A faster. If the child or other member of his family won, the spirit would vanish and the family would be saved.

About the String

The Eskimos used sinew or a leather thong to make their string figures. Other peoples further south made twine from the inside of bark. We are told Tikopian children in the Pacific Islands area preferred fibre from the hibiscus tree, although they would use a length of fishing line if it was handy. Some people even used human hair, finely braided.

Fortunately, you don't have to go out into the woods or cut your hair to get a good string for making string figures.

You can use ordinary white butchers' string knotted together at the ends. Macrame cord also works quite well, as it is thicker than string. A thicker string loop will better show off your string figures.

Dressmakers' supply stores sell nylon cord (usually by the metre). This kind of cord is probably the best, and because it is woven, not plied or twisted, it won't crease. It can be joined without a knot. A knot in your string loop can cause tangles, and figures that move won't go smoothly if there is a knot in the way.

How to Make Your String

You need about two metres of string or cord, so that your string loop will measure one metre when it is joined. This is a standard size. If this length seems uncomfortably long, a shorter string is fine for most of the figures.

The string can be either tied or melted together.

To Tie Your String

You need a knot that won't slip, so a square knot is best.

1.
Lay the right end of the string across the left end.

2.
Put this right end under the left string to tie the first part of the knot.

3.
Lay the new left end across the new right end.

4.
Put this new left end under the new right string and tighten the knot.

5.
Trim the ends to make the knot neat.

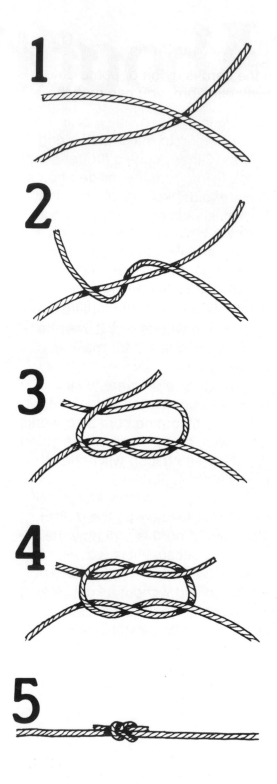

To Melt Your String

If the cord is nylon or some other synthetic fibre, you can melt the ends together. Joining the string takes practice, and it has to be done quickly while the cord is hot. You will probably need some help, so please do this with an adult.

1.
Hold the ends of the string near each other, about one or two centimetres above a candle flame. If the ends are not melting at all, they are too far away from the flame. They will singe if you are holding them too close.

2.
When the ends are gooey, stick them together.

3.
Count to five to let them cool, then roll them between your fingers to smooth the joint.

You have now made your "play string" or "ayahaak" as the Eskimos call it.

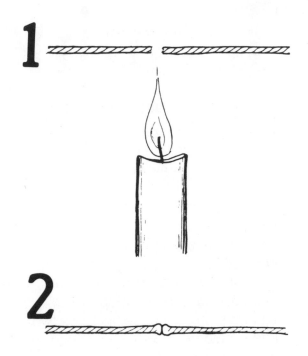

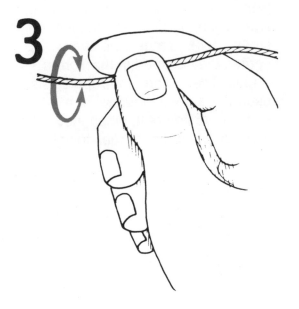

Terminology

There's a Special Language

A long time ago, people made lists of the names of string figures, or brought back drawings of the finished patterns. Some even kept the string pattern itself, fastened to a piece of paper.

But once a string figure is finished, it is almost impossible to tell just how it was made. We can learn and teach each other string figures today because, in 1898, two anthropologists, Dr A. C. Haddon and Dr W. H. R. Rivers, invented a special language to describe the way string figures are made. Haddon and Rivers developed their special language to record all the steps it took to make the string figures they learned in the Torres Straits. Then, other anthropologists used this same language, or a simpler version of it, when they wanted to remember the string figures they saw in their travels.

The language used in this book to describe the making of the figures is similar to that used by Haddon and Rivers. The loops and the strings have names, and there are also names for some of the basic positions and moves.

About Loops

When the string goes around your finger or thumb, it makes a **loop**.

The loops take their names from their location on your hands: **thumb loop, index loop, middle finger loop, ring finger loop, little finger loop**.

If you move a loop from one finger to another, it gets a new name: a loop that was on your thumb but is now on your little finger is a new little finger loop.

Each loop has a **near string** — the one nearer (or closer) to you — and a **far string** — the one farther from you.

If there are two loops on your thumb or finger, one is the **lower loop** — the one near the base of your thumb or finger — and the other is the **upper loop** — the one near the top of your thumb or finger. Don't get these loops mixed up, and be sure to keep them apart.

About Making the Figures

As you make the figures in this book, you will be weaving the strings of the loops on your fingers. Your fingers or thumbs can go over or under the strings to pick up one or more strings, then go back to the basic position.

Sometimes you may **drop** or **release** a loop from your fingers.

It takes a little while to get used to holding your hands so that the strings don't drop off your fingers. If you accidentally drop a loop or a string, it is best to start all over again.

Now go and get your string —let's begin!

Names of the Strings

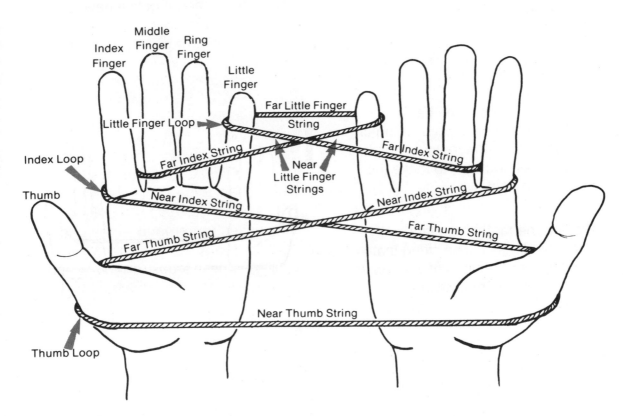

The Basic Position

Your hands begin in the **basic position** for most string figures and usually return to the basic position after each move.

1.
Your hands are parallel, the palms are facing each other, and your fingers are pointing up.

The hands in some of the pictures are not in the basic position. The hands are shown with the palms facing you so that you can see all the strings clearly.

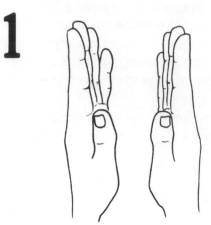

Position 1

1.
With your hands in the basic position, hang the loop of string on your thumbs. Stretch your hands as far apart as you can, to make the string loop tight.

2.
Pick up the far thumb string with your little fingers. The string that goes across the palm of your hand is called the **palmar string**.

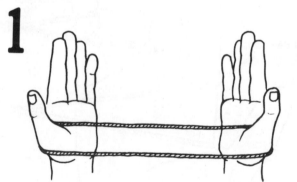

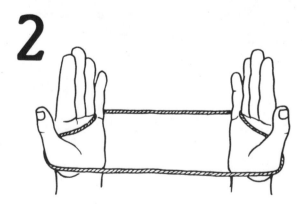

Opening A

Many string figures begin with
Opening A.

1.
Put the string loop on your fingers in
Position 1.
With your right index finger, pick up
from below the palmar string on
your left hand, and return to the
basic position pulling this string on
the back of your index finger as far
as it will go.

2.
With your left index finger, pick up
the right palmar string, from below,
in between the strings of the loop
that goes around your right index
finger. Return to the basic position,
again pulling out the palmar string as
far as it will go.

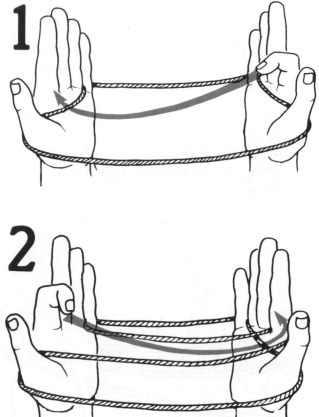

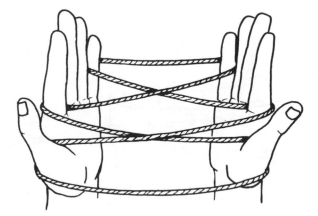

To Navaho a Loop

When you have two loops on your thumb or finger, a lower loop and an upper loop, you **Navaho** these loops by lifting the lower loop — with the thumb and index finger of your opposite hand, or with your teeth — up over the upper loop and over the tip of your finger or thumb.

You can also Navaho a loop by tipping down your thumb or finger, letting the lower loop slip off, then straightening up your thumb or finger again.

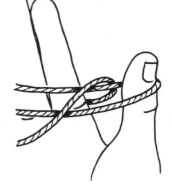

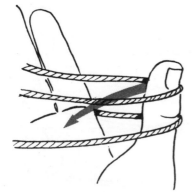 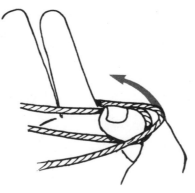

To Extend a Figure

Sometimes the strings may be woven and a figure may be finished, but it needs to be **extended** by pulling the hands apart, or by turning or twisting the hands in a certain way. Extending the figure makes a tangle of strings magically turn into a beautiful pattern.

To Take the Figure Apart

Always take the figures apart gently, as tugging creates knots. If the figure has top and bottom straight strings which frame the pattern, pull these apart and the pattern will dissolve.

To Share a Loop

Sometimes you will **share a loop** between two fingers or a finger and your thumb. You use your opposite index finger and thumb to pull out the loop so that the other finger or thumb will fit into the loop as well.

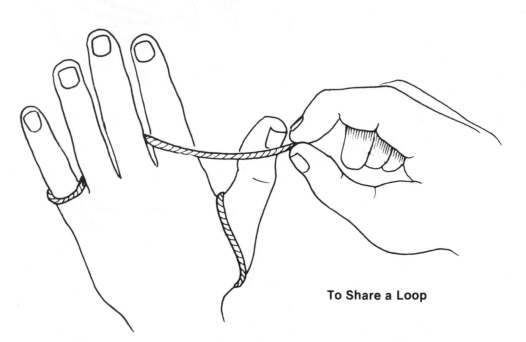

To Share a Loop

Getting a String or Strings

When the instructions tell you to **get** a string or strings, your finger or thumb goes under that string, picks up that string on its back (the back of your finger or thumb is the side with the fingernail); then returns to the basic position carrying the string with it. The instructions will tell you if you are to use your fingers or thumb to pick up the strings in a different way.

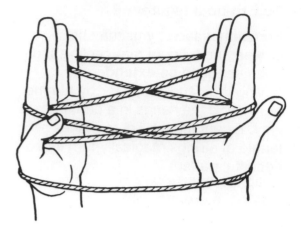

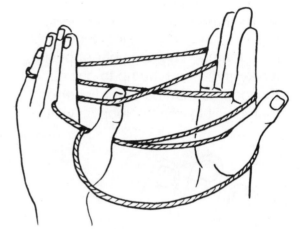

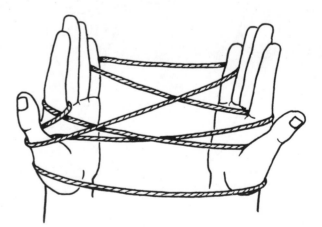

How to Double a String

For some figures, you can use a short string loop, or you can double your long string.

1.
Hang the string loop over the fingers but not the thumb of your hand.

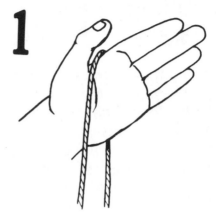

2.
Wrap the back string of the hanging loop once around your hand.

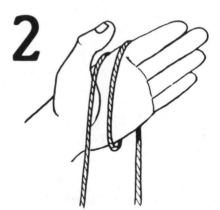

3.
Take hold of everything that crosses the palm of your hand (the loop and one hanging string) and pull these strings out as far as they will go.

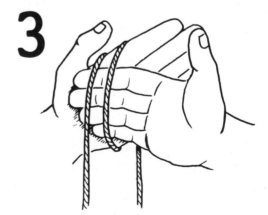

The Fish Spear

This string figure represented a fish spear or harpoon to the people who lived in the Torres Straits between Australia and New Guinea, a duck spear in Alaska, and a coconut palm tree in Africa. The Salish Indians call it Pitching a Tent. You can call it a witch's broom, especially at Hallowe'en!

1

Do Position 1.

2.
Your right index finger goes under the left palmar string and pulls it out a little bit.

3.
Your right index finger **twists its loop**. (See instructions below on How to Twist a Loop.)
Do it again. There are now two twists in the strings of the right index loop.

How to twist a loop

Rotate your index finger away from you, down, towards you and up. Make sure the twist is in the string loop, not around your index finger.

4.
Your right index finger pulls out its twisted loop as far as it will go.

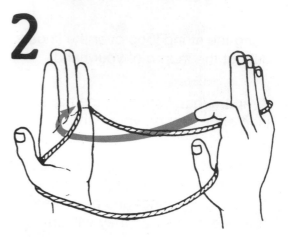

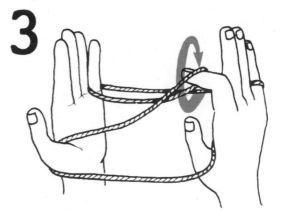

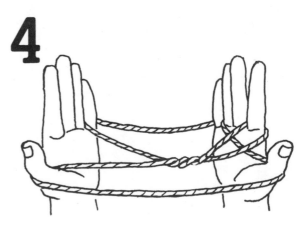

5

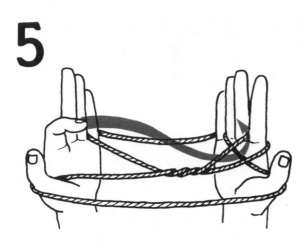

5.
Your left index finger picks up, from below, the right palmar string between the strings of the right index loop. Now pull this loop out as far as it will go.

6.
Your right thumb and right little finger drop their loops. Pull your right index finger out as far as it will go so that the loops move up the string towards your left hand.

7.
Now you've made the Fish Spear.

6

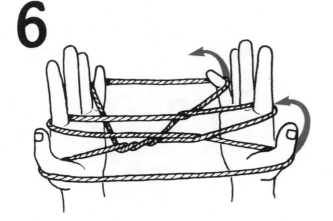

7

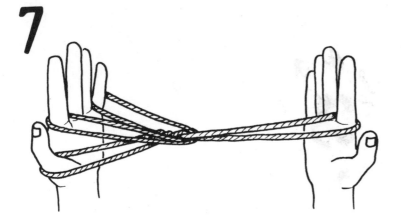

Winking Eye

This string figure came from the Hawaiian island of Kauai. Use your imagination and you can really see the eye wink.

1.
Hang the string loop over the fingers (but not the thumb) of your left hand. Your left middle, ring and little fingers close on the string hanging down across the palm of your hand. Your index finger still points out.

2.
Your right index finger and thumb take the back string of the hanging loop, wrap it all the way around your left index finger, then bring it forward to hang up on your thumb.

3.
Your right index finger and thumb pull out the loop around your left index finger to share it with your left thumb. Be careful not to twist the loop when you do this.

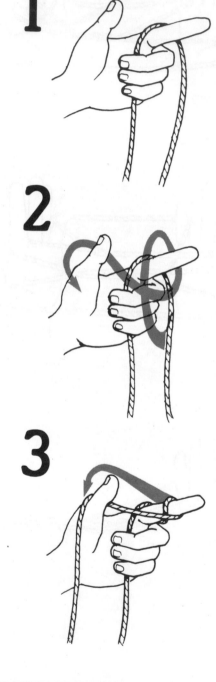

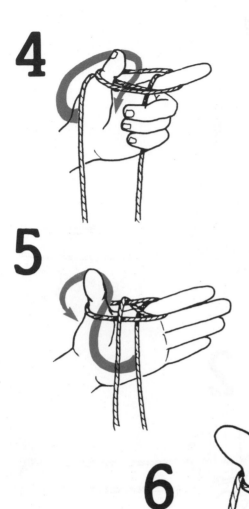

4.
Take the string of the hanging loop which is nearest to you, lift it up over the string which runs between your index finger and thumb, and let it hang down in front of this string between your index finger and thumb.

5.
Take the other string of the hanging loop (the one you have been holding) and lift it up to hang over your thumb.

How to make the Eye wink

6.
To close the eye, pull sideways on the strings of the hanging loop, and let your left index finger and thumb come closer together. To open the eye, pull your left index finger and thumb farther apart and loosen your hold on the strings of the hanging loop.

The Saw

This figure of the saw is found in many parts of the world. This is the way people in Scotland made it. As they sawed, they chanted:
See saw, Johnnie Maw,
See san, Johnnie Man.

1.
Put the string loop behind the index, middle, and ring fingers of each hand.

2.
With the index finger and thumb of your right hand, take the near string of the loop around the fingers of your left hand and wrap it once around your left index, middle, and ring fingers. With the index finger and thumb of your left hand, take the near string of the loop around the fingers of your right hand and wrap it once around the index, middle, and ring fingers of your right hand.

3.
Now complete as in Opening A using your middle fingers.

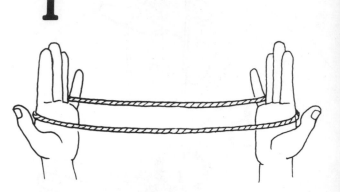

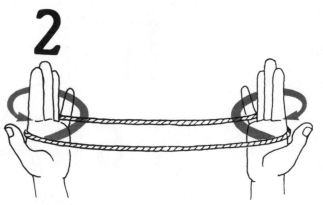

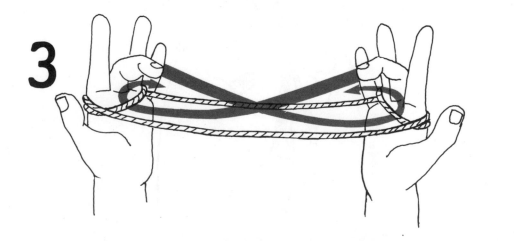

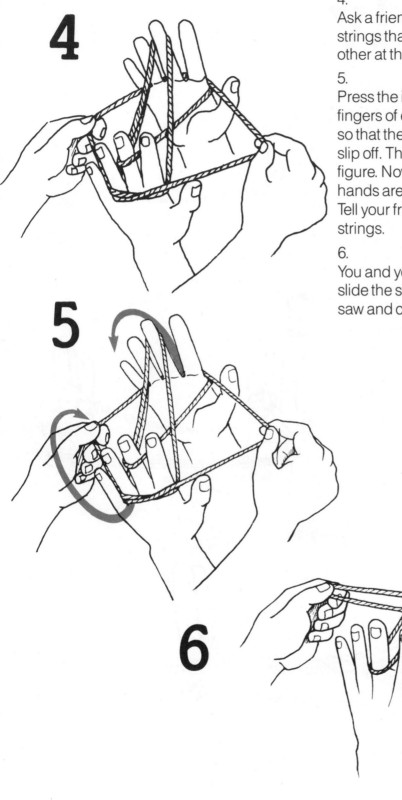

4.
Ask a friend to take hold of the long strings that run from one hand to the other at the bottom of the figure.

5.
Press the index, middle, and ring fingers of each hand tightly together so that the middle finger loops don't slip off. Then take your hands out of the figure. Now, the only loops on your hands are around your middle fingers. Tell your friend to hang on to his/her strings.

6.
You and your friend can now easily slide the strings back and forth like a saw and chant the verse.

The Fly

This version of the Fly comes from the Solomon Islands which are near New Guinea in the Pacific Ocean. It was also known as a mosquito, a locust, and even a flying fox.

You clap your hands together to try and catch that fly, but when you pull your hands apart, you'll find the fly has escaped again. Maybe your friends will have better luck!

1

1.
Hang the string loop on your little fingers. Your thumbs get both strings of the little finger loops.

2.
Your right index finger gets the two left palmar strings.

3.
Your left thumb goes over the far index strings to pick up from below, the two right palmar strings, not between but beside, the strings of the right index loop.

2

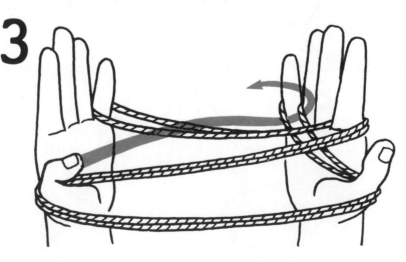

3

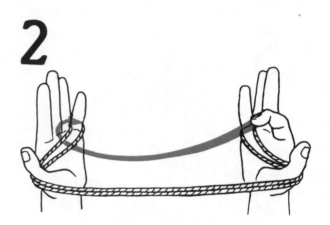

4

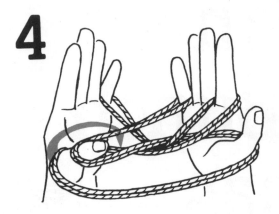

5

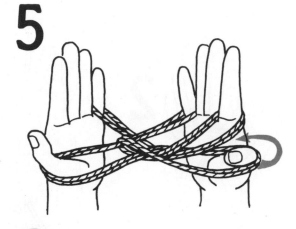

6

4.
Navaho the left thumb loops.

5.
Your right thumb drops its loops. Now, pull the strings tight.

6.
Your left thumb and right index finger drop their loops to release the fly's wings. Don't pull with your little fingers yet.

7.
You clap your hands to catch the fly. Your little fingers now pull out their loops to show that the fly is gone.

7

The Hogan and the Bunch of Bananas

This figure represents a Navaho tent, which is called a Hogan. It also makes a bunch of bananas. Are you hungry?

1.
Hang the string loop around the back of the index and middle fingers of your left hand. The long loop hangs down across your palm. Your right index finger goes into the hanging loop from behind, then between your left index and middle finger. Use this finger like a hook to take hold of the string that goes behind your left index and middle fingers. Pull this loop out as far as it will go, letting the string loop slide off your wrist. Let go of the string.

2.
Your right hand goes into the long hanging loop from below. Your right thumb and index finger take hold of the strings which go between your left index and middle finger. Make sure to pick them up above the single front loop.

3.
Pull out these strings as far as they will go, letting the wrist loop slide off your right hand as you pull. Keep holding the loop with your right thumb and index finger. Be careful not to twist the loop.

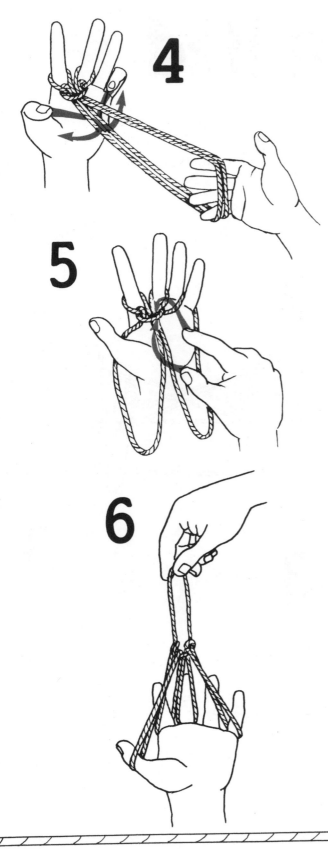

Now make this loop wider by putting the rest of the fingers of your right hand into the loop.

This double string loop has two top strings (the strings that run between your left index and middle finger), and two bottom strings.

4.
Your left thumb and little finger each take, from below, one of the bottom strings. Drop the strings held by your right hand.

5.
There is a small loop that goes around the loops on your left index and middle fingers. With your right thumb and index finger, gently pull out this small loop. Don't pull too far or the figure will fall apart.

6.
This is the Navaho Hogan.

7.
When you take the fingers of your left hand out of their loops, you have the Bunch of Bananas. See if your friends can pick one banana without taking the whole bunch.

Man on a Bed

This figure comes from the Torres Straits. After you have made the Man on a Bed, chant:
Man on a bed, man on a bed
Lies asleep, lies asleep,
The bed breaks.
When the bed breaks, the man falls out!

1

Do Opening A. Keep the index loops near the tips of your index fingers.

2.
Your thumbs go under the index loops to get the near little finger strings and return under the strings of the index loops.

3.
Your little fingers hook down the far index strings. Your little fingers get the far thumb strings. They return through the strings of the index loops.

2

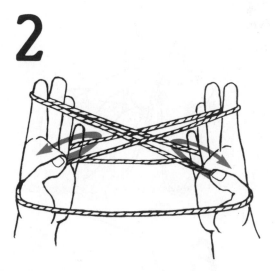

3

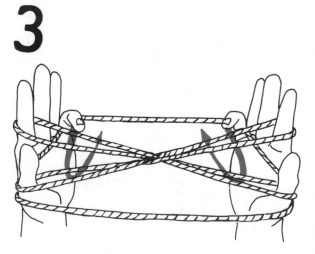

4

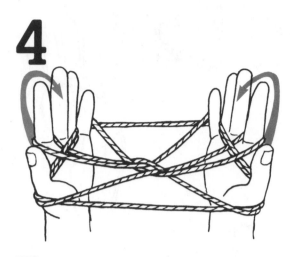

4.
Your index fingers drop their loops to make. . .

5.
. . .the Man on a Bed.

To make the bed break, drop both loops from your little fingers and pull with your thumbs.

5

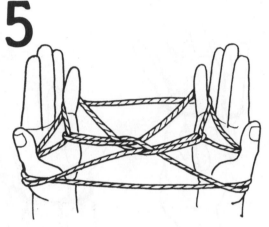

How to make the Hoochie Koochie Man

Begin again, but this time put a half twist (make an X) in the string loop as you put it on your hands in Position 1. Now complete Opening A and follow steps 1 to 6. You make him dance by turning your hands so that first your thumbs and then your little fingers come close together.

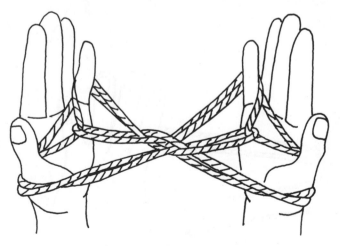

A Bird

This bird comes from Papua in New Guinea. You can make him fly across the string — but only in one direction!

1

Do Position 1 on your left hand.

2.
With your right index finger and thumb, pull out the left palmar string as far as it will go.

3.
With your right index finger and thumb, pull out the new left palmar string as far as it will go.

4.
Put your right thumb and little finger from the front, into the hanging loop. From the outside, put your right thumb into the left thumb loop and, also from the outside, put your right little finger into the left little finger loop.

5.
Use your thumb and little finger like hooks to pull these loops out as far as they will go. You have made a string triangle near your left hand.

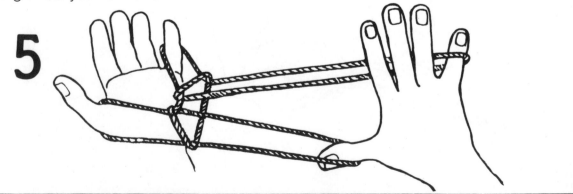

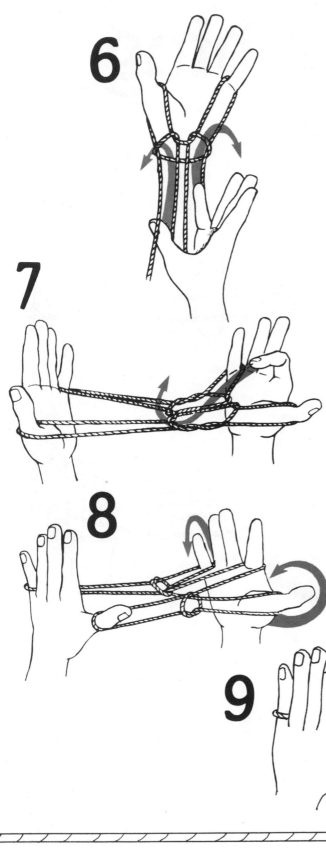

6.
Take your right thumb and little finger out of the loops they are holding. From the front, near the string triangle, put your right thumb into the hanging thumb loop, and your right little finger into the hanging little finger loop. Put these fingers up behind the string which makes the base of the string triangle.

7.
Gently draw this string out as far as it will go. Now there is a string diamond near your right hand. (If you pull too hard, the diamond, and the bird, will be too small.) There is a loop which runs out from between your left little finger and ring finger, down to the diamond and back between your left index finger and thumb. Pick up this loop inside the diamond with your right index finger.
See saw your hands away from each other to tighten the strings a little.

8.
Drop the loops from your right thumb and little finger (these loops are the wings).

9.
Pull with your right index finger to make the bird fly along the string.

Man Climbing a Tree

Someone looked at a drawing of this completed figure and worked backwards through all the steps to recreate the man climbing the tree. This is one string puzzle that was solved! Man Climbing a Tree is an Australian original. You will see that the higher the man climbs, the smaller he gets.

1

Do Opening A.

2.

Turn your hands so that your palms are facing you. Your little fingers go over all the strings to get the near thumb string and then return.

3.

Each little finger now has two loops. You want to Navaho these loops. Make sure that the new far little finger string (the one you just picked up from your thumbs), stays above the old far little finger string.

Your right index finger and thumb pick up the lower far little finger string near your left little finger, carry it over the top of your left little finger, and let it lie in the centre of the figure.

Your left index finger and thumb pick

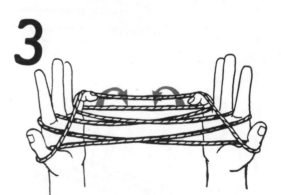

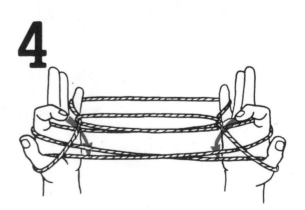

5

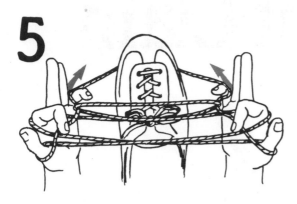

6

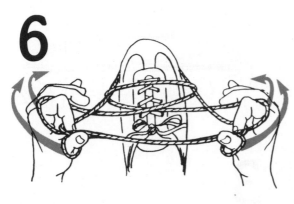

7

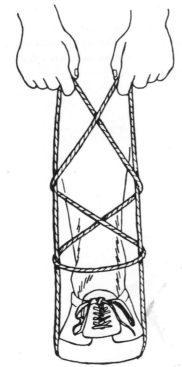

up the lower far little finger string near your right little finger, carry it over the top of your right little finger, and let it lie in the centre of the figure.

The loops you have just Navahoed must stay on the far side of the index loops.

4.
There is a palmar string which crosses each index loop. Hook your index fingers over these strings and down into the index loops.

5.
Put your foot into the big loop held by your little fingers, and take your little fingers out.

6.
Now drop the loops from your thumbs. Each thumb can push off the opposite thumb loop, but hold on tightly to the strings under your index fingers as you do this. The loops on your index fingers will slip off by themselves.

7.
Pull gently with your index fingers and you will see the man with his arms and legs wrapped around the tree. To make him climb the tree, pull gently with your right index finger, then with your left. As you keep doing this, he will climb higher and higher.

The Giant Clam

The Giant Clam comes from Fiji in the South Pacific. It opens and shuts when you seesaw your hands back and forth. This is one string figure that you can use as a kind of puppet.

1

Do Opening A.

2.
Your thumbs drop their loops. Pull the strings out until they are tight.

3.
Your right thumb goes over and holds down the strings of the right index loop and the right near little finger string. Turn your palm away from you and point your thumb down to make this move easier.

4.
Your right index finger hooks down over the right far little finger string. Now your right thumb can release the strings it was holding down. As you straighten up your index finger, turn the palm of your right hand towards you so that the far little finger string can curve around the back of your index finger to become a new right upper index loop. Keep these index loops separate, the upper loop high on your index finger.

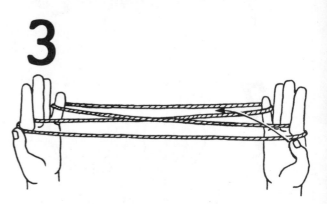

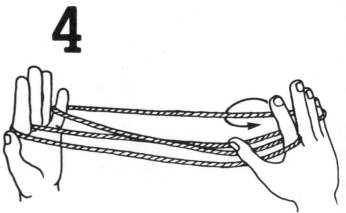

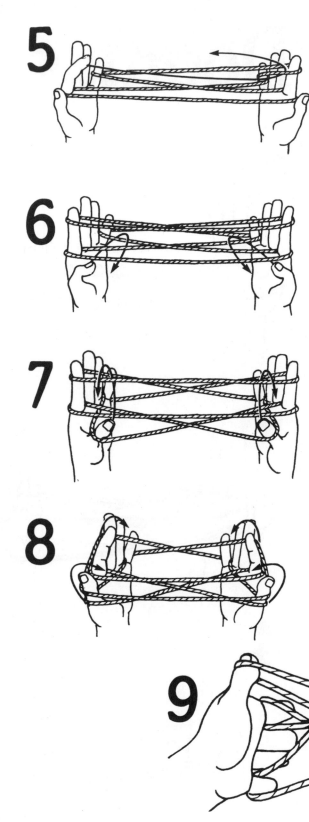

5.
Your left index finger goes, from below, up into this new upper right index loop and pulls it out as you return your hands to the basic position. This loop is now shared between the index fingers.

6.
Your thumbs go under the strings of both sets of index loops to get the near little finger strings. Return under the strings of the index loops.

7.
Your thumbs now go up into the upper index loops to share them.

8.
Navaho the thumb loops with your fingers or your teeth, then let the upper index loops slip off your index fingers. Be sure to keep the lower index loops.

9.
This is the Giant Clam. You can make it open and close and carry on conversations by seesawing your hands sideways so that first your thumbs, then your little fingers come close together.

Apache Door

This is a Navaho figure which shows the decorated door flap of an Apache tent. It is longer and more difficult than many of the other figures in this book, but the finished pattern is very beautiful. Don't forget to rub your hands together to summon the magic which will make the figure appear.

1

Do Position 1.

2.

Put your whole right hand under the left palmar string and as you pull it out, let the string loop slide down around your right wrist.

3.

Put your whole left hand, thumb too, under the right palmar string and, as you pull it out, let the string loop slide down around your left wrist.

4.

Your thumbs get the near little finger strings and return.

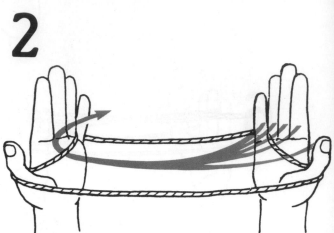

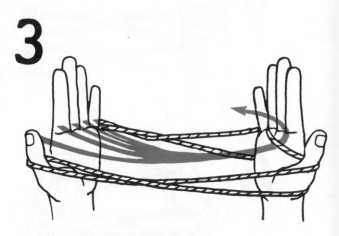

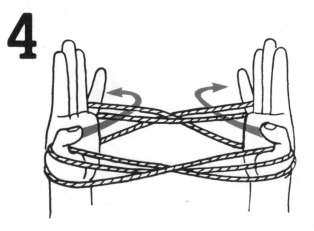

5

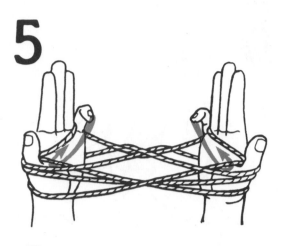

6

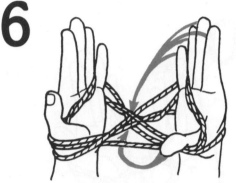

7

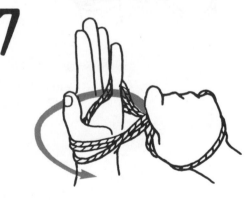

8a

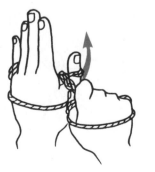

b

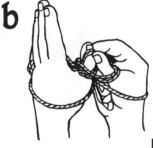

5.
Your little fingers get the far thumb strings and return.

6.
With your whole right hand, take hold of all the strings in the middle of the figure.

7.
Put all these strings between your left index finger and thumb. Make sure these strings don't cover up the thumb loops — you'll need these. Then let go of the strings you are holding with your right hand.

8.
Now, use your right index finger and thumb to take hold of the two left thumb loops and hang on to them. Don't move this right hand at all.

Keep going…

33

9.
Take your left thumb out of these two thumb loops and out of the strings you have just wrapped around it. From below, slide your left thumb back into the two loops that your right index finger and thumb have been holding.

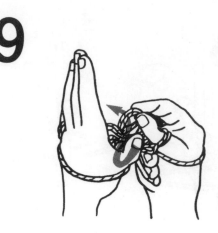

10.
Repeat this for your right hand. So, with your left hand, take hold of all the strings in the middle of the figure.

11.
Put all these strings between your right index finger and thumb.

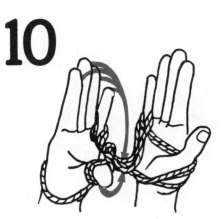

12.
With your left index finger and thumb, take hold of the two right thumb loops and hang on to them. Remember not to move your left hand.

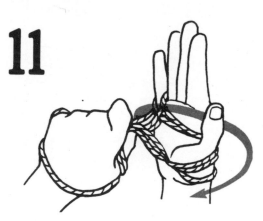

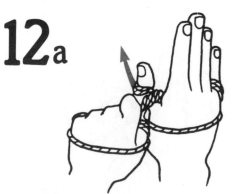

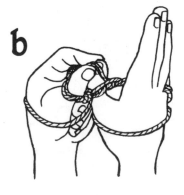

13

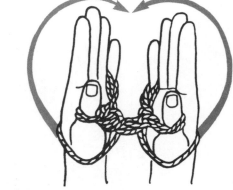

13.
Take your right thumb out of these two thumb loops and out of the strings you have just wrapped around it. From below, slide your right thumb back into the loops held by your left index and thumb.

14.
With your right index finger and thumb, take the left wrist loop right off your left hand and let it lie in the middle of the figure. With your left index finger and thumb, take the right wrist loop right off your right hand and let it lie in the middle of the figure.

15.
Now comes the most important part. Put your hands together and rub the strings to summon the magic you will need to make the figure appear.

16.
Extend the figure by pulling your hands apart. For best results, see saw your hands up and down a little as you do this.

14

15

16

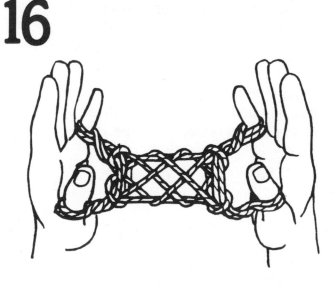

Cat's Cradle

The game of Cat's Cradle probably travelled from Asia to Europe with the tea trade in the seventeenth century. We know that children in England played Cat's Cradle as early as 1782, because a writer named Charles Lamb talked about weaving "cat-cradles" with his friends when he was at school.

To play this game, you need two people (A and B). In most Cat's Cradle figures, you can see X's and straight strings.

One person holds the figure while the other picks up the X's and takes them over, under, or between the straight strings. The players take turns holding the figure and picking up the X's to move to the next step.

The game can go on forever, but if you want to stop, you can end at the Crowns, figure 8.

There are many different ways to pick up the X's, so keep playing and keep experimenting.

Note:
As you play the game, make sure you are holding your strings securely before your partner takes his/her hands out of the figure.

Cat's Cradle 1

The Cradle (A makes the Cradle)

1.
Put the string loop around the backs of the fingers (but not the thumb) of each hand.

2.
Your right index finger and thumb pick up the near string of the loop around your left hand and wrap it once around your left hand. The string comes out between your left index finger and thumb.
Your left index finger and thumb pick up the near string of the loop around your right hand and wrap it once around your right hand. Make sure you always pick up the **near** string. One near and one far string wrapped around will give you tangled candles later on.

3.
Now complete as in Opening A using your middle fingers.

4.
The completed cradle.

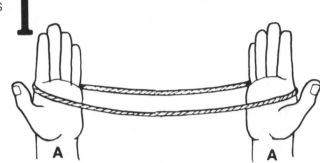

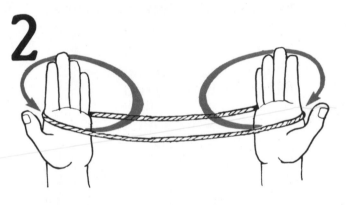

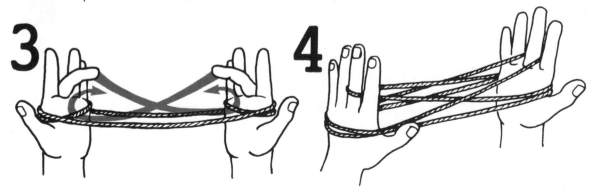

Cat's Cradle 2

The Cradle to Soldier's Bed (B makes the Bed)

1.
Your index fingers and thumbs take hold of the X's at the sides of the figure.

2.
Pull the X's out to the sides.

3.
Push the X's down and take them under the long side framing strings at the bottom of the figure. Now, turn your index fingers and thumbs up.

4.
Separate your index fingers and thumbs to make the Bed.

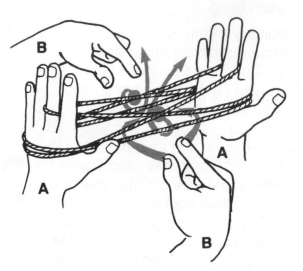

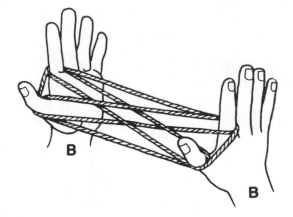

Cat's Cradle 3

Soldier's Bed to Candles (A makes Candles)

1.
Your index fingers and thumbs take the long X's.

2.
Pull the X's up, out past the framing strings of the figure.

3.
Push the X's down and under the straight framing strings. Now, turn your index fingers and thumbs up.

4.
Separate your index fingers and thumbs to make Candles.

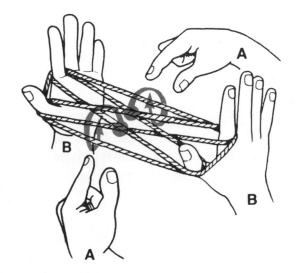

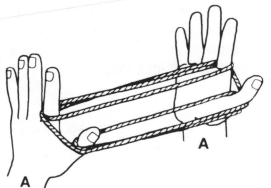

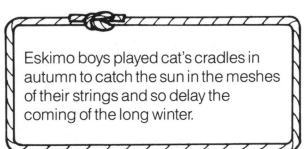

Eskimo boys played cat's cradles in autumn to catch the sun in the meshes of their strings and so delay the coming of the long winter.

Cat's Cradle 4

Candles to Manger (B makes the Manger)

1.
Use your left little finger, face up, like a hook, to get the far thumb candle string and pull it across the figure out past the far index strings. Hang on to this string.

2.
Then, use your right little finger, face up, like a hook, to get the near index candle string and pull it across the figure out past the near thumb strings.

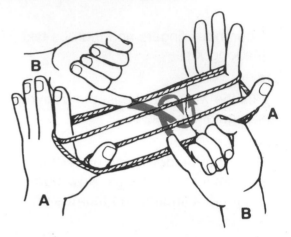

3.
Now, your right index finger and thumb go down into the string triangle between the framing strings of the figure and the string held by your right little finger. In the same way, your left index finger and thumb go down into the string triangle held by your left little finger.

4.
Your index fingers and thumbs go under, then pick up on their backs, the straight framing strings of the figure.

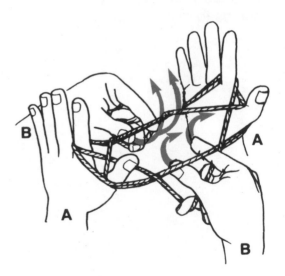

5.
Continue to hold the little finger strings securely and separate your index fingers and thumbs to make the Manger.

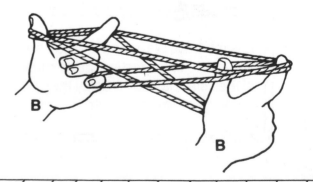

Cat's Cradle 5

Manger to Diamonds (A makes Diamonds)

1.
Your index fingers and thumbs take the long X's at the sides of the figure.

2.
Pull the X's out, then up.

3.
Now, take the X's across and over the top framing strings of the figure and point your index fingers and thumbs down into the centre of the figure.

4.
Separate your index fingers and thumbs to make Diamonds.

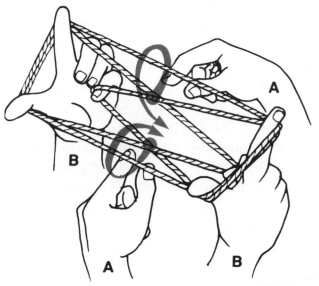

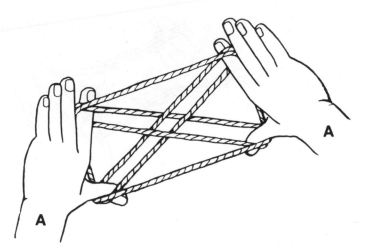

Cat's Cradle 6

Diamonds to Cat's Eye (B makes Cat's Eye)

1.
Your index fingers and thumbs take
the long X's.

2.
Pull them up and out past the
framing strings of the figure.

3.
Now push them down and under the
straight framing strings, and turn
your index fingers and thumbs up.

4.
Separate your index fingers and
thumbs to make Cat's Eye.

Sometimes, Papuans used cat's
cradle strings to tie new yam shoots to
their supporting sticks. Magically, the
yam shoots would twine around their
sticks the way the strings had twined
around their fingers.

Cat's Cradle 7

Cat's Eye to Fish in a Dish (A makes Fish in a Dish)

1.
Your index fingers and thumbs go down into the loops held by B's index fingers and thumbs, and pinch the sides of the central diamond where they meet the framing strings.

2.
Turn your index fingers and thumbs up into the large central diamond of the figure.

3.
Separate your index fingers and thumbs to make Fish in a Dish.

You can end the game here by making the Crowns, (figure 8). If you want to continue, go on to make Hand Drum (figure 9).

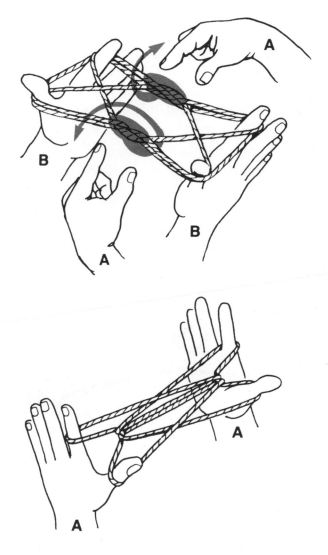

Mystery Figure

What figure do you get when you take the X's up into the centre of the figure from below, between the two straight central strings?

Cat's Cradle 8

Fish in a Dish to Two Royal Crowns
(B makes Two Royal Crowns and ends the game)

1.
Your index fingers and thumbs take the long X's and pull them out to the sides to make the Crowns.

This figure is also called Grandfather Clock.

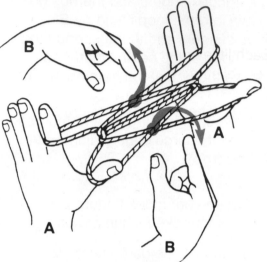

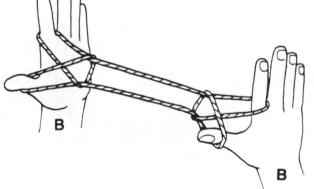

Cat's Cradle 9

Fish in a Dish to Hand Drum (B makes the Drum)

This time, the X's are on the outside and the straight strings are in the centre.

1.
Each little finger takes the straight central string nearest to it and pulls it out past the X's. Hang on to these strings. There is now a central diamond framed by the X's.

2.
Now, your index fingers and thumbs take the X's as usual.

3.
Still holding the little finger strings, turn your index fingers and thumbs up into the central diamond.

4.
Separate your index fingers and thumbs to complete the Hand Drum.

You can end the game here by making the Lucky Tea Kettle (figure 11), or go on to make Diamonds (figure 10).

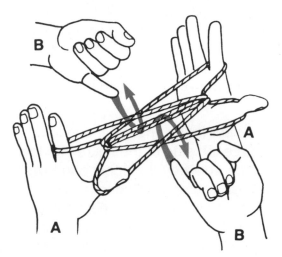

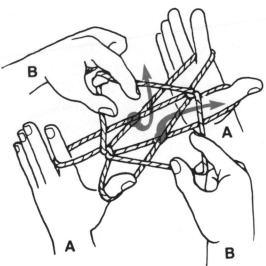

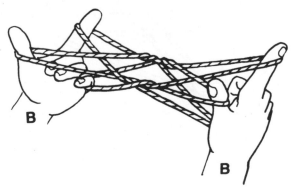

Cat's Cradle 10

Hand Drum to Diamonds (A makes Diamonds)

First, you have to find the X's. The strings that make the X's run up from B's little fingers. The figure has two lower loops held by B's little fingers, and four upper loops held by B's index fingers and thumbs.

1.
Put your index fingers and thumbs from each side of the figure into the space between the upper and lower loops. Your index fingers and thumbs are touching the strings of both little finger loops. Slide your index fingers and thumbs towards each other along the strings of the little finger loops until they close on the strings that lace together in the middle of each side of the figure. When you pull these strings out to the sides, the X's should come free, leaving only two straight framing strings.

2.
Your index fingers and thumbs pull the X's out to the sides.

3.
Now, take the X's towards each other over the framing strings.

4.
Turn your index fingers and thumbs down into the centre space of the figure.

5.
Separate your index fingers and thumbs to make Diamonds.

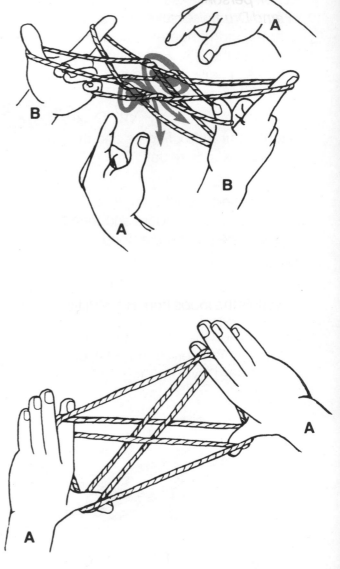

Cat's Cradle 11

Hand Drum to the Lucky Tea Kettle

(It takes three people to make the Lucky Tea Kettle. Go and call a friend.)

In Japan, they end the game this way. Each person takes two loops of the Hand Drum figure.

1.
B is holding the Drum and keeps the loops on his/her index fingers.

2.
A takes the loops from B's left little finger and thumb.

3.
C takes the loops from B's right little finger and thumb.

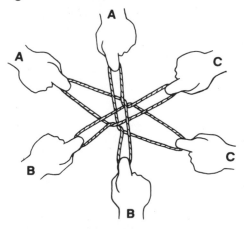

This is the Hibachi on which the Lucky Tea Kettle is put to boil. But, according to the Japanese fairy tale, the Lucky Tea Kettle is no ordinary tea kettle. It is, in fact, a talented badger tea kettle named Bumbuku-Chagama. When the kettle becomes a badger, his head with two bright eyes looks out of the spout, and four brown hairy paws and a bushy tail appear. You can imagine the clatter and clang as the Lucky Tea Kettle, complaining loudly, jumps off the fire!

To end the game, the three people holding the strings of the Hibachi, shout "Chan-garagara!" which is the noise of the tea kettle jumping off the fire. Then they all let go of their strings at once. The one left holding the strings loses the game.

ANGUS & ROBERTSON PUBLISHERS

*Unit 4, Eden Park, 31 Waterloo Road,
North Ryde, NSW, Australia 2113, and
16 Golden Square, London W1R 4BN,
United Kingdom*

*First published in Canada
by Kids Can Press in 1983
First published in Australia
by Angus & Robertson Publishers in 1986
First published in the United Kingdom
by Angus & Robertson (UK) Ltd in 1986
Published by arrangement with Kids Can Press
Reprinted 1987*

*National Library of Australia
Cataloguing-in-publication data.*

*Gryski, Camilla, 1948-
  Cat's cradle & other string games. Book II.
  ISBN 0 207 15271 3.*

  *1. String figures — Juvenile literature. 2. Games —
  Juvenile literature. I. Sankey, Tom. II. Title.*
793'.9

*Cover illustration by Louis Silvestro
Printed in Singapore*